## *Dear Parent:*
## *Your child's love of readin*

Every child learns to read in a different way and at his or her own speed. Some go back and forth between reading levels and read favorite books again and again. Others read through each level in order. You can help your young reader improve and become more confident by encouraging his or her own interests and abilities. From books your child reads with you to the first books he or she reads alone, there are I Can Read Books for every stage of reading:

**SHARED READING**
Basic language, word repetition, and whimsical illustrations, ideal for sharing with your emergent reader

**BEGINNING READING**
Short sentences, familiar words, and simple concepts for children eager to read on their own

**READING WITH HELP**
Engaging stories, longer sentences, and language play for developing readers

**READING ALONE**
Complex plots, challenging vocabulary, and high-interest topics for the independent reader

**I Can Read Books** have introduced children to the joy of reading since 1957. Featuring award-winning authors and illustrators and a fabulous cast of beloved characters, I Can Read Books set the standard for beginning readers.

A lifetime of discovery begins with the magical words **"I Can Read!"**

*Visit www.icanread.com for information on enriching your child's reading experience.*

I Can Read® and I Can Read Book® are trademarks of HarperCollins Publishers.

My Little Pony: Cutie Mark Mix-Up
MY LITTLE PONY and HASBRO and all related trademarks and logos are trademarks of Hasbro, Inc.

Printed in the United States of America.

For information address HarperCollins Children's Books, a division of HarperCollins Publishers, 195 Broadway, New York, NY 10007.
www.icanread.com

ISBN 978-0-06-306075-3
Book design by Stephanie Hays

23 24 25 26 27 LB 10 9 8 7 6 5 4 3 2 1 First Edition

# Cutie Mark Mix-Up

Based on the episode by Jim Martin
Adapted by Alexandra West

HARPER
*An Imprint of* HarperCollins*Publishers*

One beautiful day in Equestria,
pony friends Hitch and Sunny were
opening the community Garden of Magic.

Hitch was the sheriff and liked rules.

Sunny just wanted everypony to be happy.

Things were not going as planned
at the community Garden of Magic.
When Hitch and Sunny opened the gates,
all of the garden's critters escaped!

Sheriff Hitch was not happy.

He needed to get the critters to safety.

But he couldn’t do it alone.

Hitch asked his friends
Izzy, Pipp, and Zipp
to help bring the critters home.

“Then I will calm the critters down and tell them they are safe,” he said. Hitch was the only pony in the world with the power to talk to critters.

Hitch was worn-out and upset.
He visited Sunny
and their Dragon friend Sparky
at the smoothie cart.

"What a disaster," he said.

"I have the hardest job in the world."

"We all work just as hard," Sunny said.
"Smoothie carts are a lot of work.
Plus I'm an Alicorn now,
somepony everypony else looks up to."

At the same time, Sunny and Hitch said,
"You'll never understand
what it's like to be me."
Suddenly Sparky sneezed Dragonfire!

All at once, Sunny and Hitch began to act a little different. . . .

"Hey, clean up that litter!"

Sunny snapped at a nearby pony.

"Oh, relax," Hitch said.

"Let everypony do their thing!"

Pipp was the first to spot that
Sunny and Hitch were acting different.
She fluttered down to take a closer look.
That’s when she saw it!

"Don't panic," she said calmly,
"but your Cutie Marks are switched!"

Cutie Marks are unique to everypony.
They are what makes each pony special.
When Sunny and Hitch switched,
their special talents switched too!

“How hard can this sheriff thing be?”
Sunny asked.
“Definitely harder than running
a smoothie cart,” Hitch replied.

But Hitch soon found out
Sunny's job was harder than it looked.
"I'm using her recipes," he said.

"What am I doing wrong?"

"She doesn't use recipes," Zipp said. "Sunny knows everypony's order by heart."

Sunny headed to the Brighthouse
where she didn't have much
better luck as sheriff.
The critters understood her,
but they wouldn't listen to her.

“Okay, okay!” she shouted.

“Catching critters is hard!”

Back at the smoothie cart,

Zipp started to put it all together.

She realized it was Sparky's Dragonfire.

"I think I know how to fix this," she said.
"But first, Sunny needs your help!"
Hitch rushed to help his friend.

Zipp flew ahead and found Sunny.
"Hitch needs your help
at the smoothie cart!" Zipp said.
Sunny rushed to help her friend.

On their way to help, Hitch and Sunny crashed into each other!

And when they stood back up . . .

. . . their Cutie Marks were fixed!

"You were right.

Being sheriff is hard!" Sunny said.

"No, you were right!"

Hitch replied.

“Hey!” Izzy chimed in.

“We need help with these critters!”

"Let's get you critters
back where you belong," Hitch said.
The critters listened to him!

Meanwhile, Sunny went back to the smoothie cart. All of Maretime Bay was happy to have their orders right again.

"Looks like we both did pretty well," Sunny said.

"Yeah, when we each started doing what we're good at!" Hitch smiled.